Amazing Animal Adventures

In the Desert

with Brian Keating

A Snake Escape

Desert on Ice

Coyote Laughter and Newspaper Rock

Walking a Tarantula

Saskatchewan: "A Snake Escape"

Canada

Greenland

Arctic Ocean

Utah: "Coyote Laughter and Newspaper Rock"

Somerset Island: "Desert on Ice"

Europe

North America

United States

Arizona: "Walking a Tarantula"

Atlantic Ocean

Af

Baja: "A Desert Full of Whales"

Equator

A Desert Full of Whales

South America

Namibia: "Like Toothpaste from the Sand"

Pacific Ocean

Botswana: "The Okavango's Termite Islands"

Souther Ocea

Like Toothpaste from the Sand

The Okavango's Termite Islands

BRIAN KEATING'S AMAZING ANIMAL ADVENTURES

TABLE OF CONTENTS

INTRODUCTION: A NATURALIST IS BORN	4
WALKING A TARANTULA	6
THE OKAVANGO'S TERMITE ISLANDS	10
A DESERT FULL OF WHALES	14
LIKE TOOTHPASTE FROM THE SAND	18
DESERT ON ICE	22
COYOTE LAUGHTER AND NEWSPAPER ROCK	26
A SNAKE ESCAPE	32
UPSIDE-DOWN GALAHS DOWN UNDER	36
RETURNING NATURE'S CATTLE	40
CONSERVATION RESOURCES	46
INDEX	47

Asia

Indian Ocean

Pacific Ocean

Australia

Simpson Desert: "Upside-down Galahs Down Under"

mbabwe: "Returning Nature's Cattle"

Returning Nature's Cattle

Upside-down Galahs Down Under

ntarctic Continent

N

0   1500   3000 km

A NATURALIST IS BORN

I was born in Medicine Hat, Alberta, and spent the first six years of my life there before moving to New York State. I don't remember a lot from those early years, but I do remember the smells of sage, dry prairie air, and ranches. I can remember walking along dusty trails, playing with my brothers in the coulees, and going fishing for suckers

Climbing a vine in Zimbabwe

for the first time with my father at a little trickle of creek. All of these memories are from my years in Medicine Hat, which technically isn't a desert but its close, with only about 33 centimeters (13 in.) of precipitation every year.

My dryland upbringing has allowed me to relate well to the desert as an adult. When I became a naturalist, I worked first in the wetlands of British Columbia, then at the Prairie Wildlife Centre near Swift Current, Saskatchewan. Getting that job was like going home. I was paid to bird-watch, to look for wildlife, and to interpret the prairie ecology to visitors who didn't understand the prairies. I rented an old homestead from a farm family, the Schaeffers. The Schaeffers didn't like trees. Ed Shaeffer liked the view so he never planted a tree. Because of the treeless land all around the house, when lightning storms would occur at night, it was like the lightning was right in my bedroom. I would often open my window to experience the wind and the electric night air.

Walking back and forth to work, I got to know the dryland environment very well. I knew where all the birds were nesting and what kinds of predators those birds should be on the look-out for. I knew the plant life, too. I would try to walk a different route to work every day to find out as much as I could about the sometimes severe prairie landscape. Working at the Prairie

4

Your Own Backyard Adventure
Creating a Desert Animal

Throughout this desert book, I talk about the amazing ways plants and animals have managed to survive in such a harsh environment. It's hard to imagine that anything can grow and thrive in these places. Now it's your turn to do the imagining! What would the perfect desert animal look like? How would it live? Here's your challenge: create an animal that is well adapted to a life in the desert.

You will need:
- several pieces of paper
- colored pencil crayons, pen or pencil
- an encyclopedia or other reference materials

What to do:
After reading this book and doing some other research on desert critters, think about what makes desert animals unique. On a piece of paper, create a list of traits and features that many desert animals share. These can be both physical and behavioral adaptations. Physical adaptations are things like coloring, skin type, and size, whereas behavioral adaptations include breeding, hunting, and social habits.

Design your own desert animal that uses these strategies to survive. Does it only come out at night? Does it recycle water within its body? Does it have feet perfect for moving in sandy desert environments?

Create a color picture of your animal, complete with name and description of its traits and where it lives.

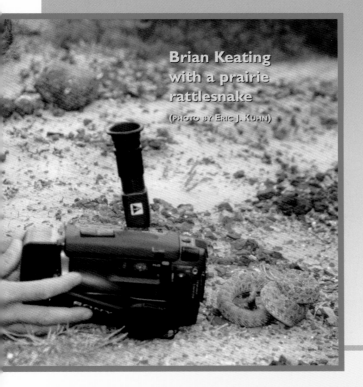

Brian Keating with a prairie rattlesnake
(PHOTO BY ERIC J. KUHN)

Wildlife Centre sharpened my interest in extreme environments, especially deserts, and how animals and plants make a living in them.

Now, with my wife, Dee, I explore all kinds of landscapes and come into contact with animals all over the world through my work with the Calgary Zoo as the director of the Conservation Outreach Program. I am just as amazed by the deserts I see now as I was by the drylands I knew in my youth. The birds, the animals, the plants—all living in such fragile places—are such complex survivors. I hope you will enjoy the stories in this book, about some of the amazing people, places, plants, and animals that have inspired me to learn more about nature and seek out the world's wild spaces. Maybe something in these stories will inspire you, too.

WALKING A TARANTULA

Shortly after I started working at the Calgary Zoo, I had the opportunity to attend a conference at the Arizona Desert Museum in Tucson. It drew people from all over North America. There was an unusual number of people in one place who were into desert animals, but perhaps hadn't spent their whole careers in a desert environment. It was exciting because the desert is right at Tucson's doorstep, and the Arizona Desert Museum is probably the best place in the world to experience and interpret the desert environment.

For me, the conference was an all-out energy expenditure. I joined the reptile guys during the night until 1:00 or 2:00 in the morning, and then I'd wake up with the birders and go bird-watching at 4:30 or 5:00 in the morning. I was getting 2 or 3 hours of sleep a night, and in between I survived on coffee, adrenalin, and 20-minute catnaps. I have great memories of being exceptionally tired but completely buzzed with excitement about the things we found.

The conference was in September and the days were very hot. Reptiles don't like to get terribly hot, so you just don't find reptiles in the heat of the day. They come out in the morning to warm up and in the evening after it has cooled down. During the daytime, many animals are deep in underground burrows, where the temperature is very pleasant and where the humidity is relatively high. In the middle of the day, the desert is a quiet, often desolate, area unless you know exactly where to look.

There are some animals that are specifically adapted for moving around during the day in the desert, like the acorn woodpecker and the roadrunner. We got brief glimpses of

A friend of mine said that the desert represents "the greatest Earth on show." Dee and I could sure understand why, especially at sunrise and sunset.

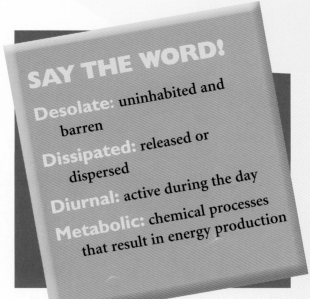

When ultraviolet light is shone on a scorpion, the light is absorbed and reflected as a greenish light. This green tinge can also be seen on the scorpion in bright sunlight. Some other creatures, like millipedes, sow bugs, and even some beetles, glow in ultraviolet light as well.

a roadrunner as it raced from one location to the next. The sighting was a highlight.

We'd go out at sunset and drive slowly. The asphalt held in the heat during the day and dissipated it during the evening. We used spotlights and our vehicles' headlights to find all kinds of species of snakes, geckos, and lizards warming up on the road. It was incredibly exciting. I remember seeing a zebra-tailed lizard dash off the side of the road, so we got out of the vehicle and pursued it with flashlights just to photograph it. We also found scorpions at night with ultraviolet lights. The scorpions glowed green!

After a late night of pursuing reptiles, I'd get up early in the morning. Dawn in the desert is spectacular. The best time of the day is right at the crack of dawn—15 minutes before sunrise to 15 minutes after. That half hour of the day is magical because that's when the nocturnal creatures are going to bed and the diurnal creatures are waking up and starting to move around. The dawn chorus is at its best, then, too. While a tropical rainforest is overwhelming with the variety and the layering of birdlife, the desert's sparse bird calls are crystal clear and sweet. It's like poetry in the landscape. When the sun comes

SAY THE WORD!

Desolate: uninhabited and barren

Dissipated: released or dispersed

Diurnal: active during the day

Metabolic: chemical processes that result in energy production

The barrel cactus flowers from July through to September. The beautiful orange, yellow, or red flowers make way for barrel-shaped fruit that deer and other animals eat. This cactus grows faster on its shady side. This causes it to tilt toward the south, which gives it the nickname "the compass cactus."

up, it lights up the saguaro cactus and the delicate tendrils and spines of some of the weird desert plants. It just creates a fantastic landscape.

My wife, Dee, joined me for a few days after the conference was over. We rented a car and put to the test what I had learned about where to go and how to look for the animals. I remember one evening we saw a hill way off in the distance, but we knew we would never find our way back to the vehicle if we set out toward it. This was long before hand-held global positioning systems that tell you exactly where on Earth you are; this was when you could get lost out there! We parked our vehicle on a dirt road and left our parking lights on so we would be able to find our way back.

Dee and I wandered around until 1:00 or 2:00 in the morning, not really paying attention to direction except by the stars. It would have been very easy to never find our camp again. Luckily, because the desert plants produce

I walked this tarantula we encountered like you might walk your hamster from one hand to the next. Its legs touching my palm felt like little dancing pipe cleaners. It was very cool!

so I carefully let it walk off my hands and continue on its way.

What a thrill it was to come across weird desert creatures. It was my first North American desert experience, and it set the tone for my future desert adventures. I've always enjoyed trying to figure out how plants and animals live in extreme environments. I guess that's what I like most about deserts. Life has somehow figured out how to survive in some of the toughest conditions on the planet. Deserts are wonderful places to visit. There's nothing in abundance, but what you find is very special.

spines rather than big fleshy leaves, no matter how far away we got from our vehicle, when we moved around, we could catch a glimpse of light twinkling through the cactus forest, so we always knew where our camp was.

We would walk long distances without seeing anything, but now and again we'd come across something exciting like a tarantula. Finding a wild tarantula is something that excites the heck out of me. I put my hand down in front of the tarantula as it was walking and I let it walk right up onto my hand, knowing in my brain that these animals don't bite unless you seriously harass them. It was absolutely awesome! I didn't want to scare the tarantula,

BRIAN'S NOTES

Many small desert rodents, such as kangaroo rats, never drink water. They create their own metabolic water. They break down the food they eat within their own system. By combining hydrogen and oxygen they create H_2O, or water. They use ingenious methods to acquire moisture.

THE OKAVANGO'S TERMITE ISLANDS

The Kalahari Desert is one of the world's most famous deserts. It's also one of Africa's largest landscapes of untracked wilderness. Another thing that's interesting about the Kalahari Desert is that at its northern end, two rivers come together to form a huge river called the Okavango River. Most rivers flow right across Africa and empty into the ocean. But this river in northern Botswana is bizarre. It flows into a desert.

What happens when you add water to a place with rich sand and abundant sunshine?

You form an oasis. The Okavango River flows into the Okavango region and creates an inland delta. The Okavango Delta is the largest inland delta in the world. When you think of deltas, you probably think of rivers flowing into the ocean, like the Mississippi Delta in the United States, or the Mackenzie Delta in Canada. They usually have huge deposits of silt and mud, lots of nutrients, and lots of marshland, so from a wildlife standpoint, these are very important areas.

Crocodiles are the most feared predators in the water of the delta. But our mokoro polers were more worried about surprise encounters with hippos on the narrow channels!

During dry years, termites take hold in an area where there's no water, and they build a little mound. That little mound gets bigger and bigger. We climbed on termite mounds in Africa that are meters tall, like this one.

I have been into the Okavango Delta many times, but on my most recent visit in 2004, it was an exceptional year for high water. It's very exciting when there's that much water because it flows all the way down to the southern part of the delta to a town called Maun. Maun is the center of Kalahari research and exploration. Everybody flies to Maun to go into the Kalahari Desert to the south, or into the Okavango Delta to the north.

We flew out of Johannesburg into Maun by commercial jet, hopped onto a little airplane, and flew in low to the central part of the Okavango Delta. It took us about 40 minutes to get there from Maun in this little airplane, and that's a long time to fly over marshland! Almost immediately upon leaving Maun we started to see water and animal tracks through the area. And then a few minutes later, it was virtually nonstop water with

BRIAN'S NOTES

Many of the islands in the Okavango Delta were formed by termites. The water comes in and floods around the termite mounds. The mounds then provide a place for plants to grow and these plants attract more plants. Gradually, the island starts to grow outward and eventually there are islands big enough to support populations of elephants and giraffes. Without termites, the Okavango would be a very different place indeed.

islands everywhere. I guess that's why the area is nicknamed the "Sea of Land, Land of Water."

The delta's water comes out of the highlands of Angola filled with all sorts of nutrient material. As the Okavango River flows, it picks up more nutrients. As soon as the river reaches the desert, it flows outward and forms this huge nutrient-rich delta that's around 15,000 square kilometers (5,800 sq. mi.) in size. The Okavango Delta pulses in May or June when it reaches its peak. This is when most of the water enters the delta from the north. About 22,000 square kilometers

More than 30,000 elephants call the Okavango Delta home. With so much vegetation in this desert oasis, the elephants really do live in a salad bowl!

(8,500 sq. mi.) of the delta can flood during the peak time in years when rainfall is heavy. Then the water starts to recede throughout the rest of the year, and it takes several months for the water to flow through the delta and reach its southernmost point.

Along the edges of the delta in places like the Savuti and the Moremi regions, we saw some of the largest populations of elephants found anywhere in the world. There are about 50,000 of them along the edges of the Okavango in Chobe National Park and the Savuti. Along with elephants, there are giraffes and lots of lions—some of the largest concentrations of lions in Africa. These lions, in the Savuti specifically, have worked out a strategy to take down elephants. We were a bit surprised to find there are actually elephant-killing lions that, during

We watched this male hornbill continually gathering food and feeding his mate, who had entombed herself within a tree cavity. Female hornbills hole up in mud enclosures with their chicks, relying on their mates to feed them through an opening in the mud wall. They break out when the chicks can feed themselves. A perfect anti-snake strategy!

12

Cheetahs are beautiful creatures that live around the Okavango Delta. These cats are the world's fastest land animals over short distances. They can race up to 90 kilometers per hour (60 MPH).

the wet season, take down giraffes, too.

We saw lots of hippos, which are important animals in this area. Without the hippos, the Okavango would be a totally different environment. They help keep the waterways moving. If they didn't, the area would become choked with papyrus. Papyrus grows in thick abundance, especially in the northern part of the Okavango because that's where the nutrients in the water are first accessed. As the plants are busy sucking out all these nutrients, they purify the water. As the water winds through the Okavango, it turns crystal clear. I could have dipped my cup in and drunk the water from the Okavango. Set against the desert sky and setting sun, this pure water creates a surreal environment.

There are people who have lived in the delta for thousands of years. They move around in mokoros, which are dugout canoes usually made from the trunk of a sausage tree, named for its sausage-shaped fruit. It's *the* way of traveling in the Okavango Delta. The boats allowed us to move silently from one place to the next. I sat there in a dugout canoe like a sack of potatoes with a poler who knows the Okavango just like we know city streets. He navigated around in this landscape of tall papyrus leaves, and the front of the boat was constantly pushing papyrus apart as we moved through.

As we glided through the water it was just impossible to believe that I was actually in the desert—a water desert. The Okavango Delta, with its desert elephants, hippo bulldozers, and termite islands, is one of the most amazing places on Earth. It truly is a sea of land, and a land of water.

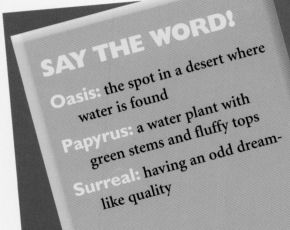

SAY THE WORD!

Oasis: the spot in a desert where water is found

Papyrus: a water plant with green stems and fluffy tops

Surreal: having an odd dream-like quality

A DESERT FULL OF WHALES

I'd never been to Mexico when we chartered a boat in San Diego and sailed down to the Baja Desert. We were lucky to be there after serious rain, so the desert was alive. It's amazing to see a usually harsh landscape so vibrant and in bloom. We saw wonderful flowers carpeting the desert floor, which was exciting and unexpected. I saw frigate birds for the first time, and the frigates and boobies—a type of gannet—were nesting on islands around Baja. We saw booby babies covered in beautiful down sitting amongst the cacti. There was some remarkable birdlife in Baja.

There was also an incredible contrast between the dry desert of Baja and the abundance found around the water. A fascinating way to explore the environment was right at the ecotone between the ocean and desert: the beach. We found interesting things washed up on the shore, like sea lion skulls and a young gray whale.

It was the first time I'd seen a dead whale and it gave me a chance to look at the baleen. Baleen is basically modified teeth. A row of keratin plates attached to the upper palate hangs down like a series of brushes. These brushes filter out the debris and allow the whales to

Dee on a hill overlooking San Ignacio Lagoon and (above) touching a gray whale. Some people argue that allowing people to touch whales could potentially transmit diseases to the whales. Some fear it could make whales too tame in areas where whales are still hunted. I maintain that getting people that close to whales and that excited about them creates whale crusaders.

I never fully understood what baleen was until I had it in my hand on the beach in Baja. I could see exactly where the whale pushed its tongue against it and frayed the baleen to create a perfect net to catch what it wanted to eat.

back-swallow food. The gray whales suck up mud like a vacuum cleaner. Then they close their mouths and push all the water and mud out with their tongue through the baleen. The baleen catches the various crustaceans that are hiding in the mud, and then the whale swallows them.

But our objective was to see *live* whales. The gray whales that feed in the shallows of the Beaufort Sea and along the Pacific coast of North America in summer come down into the desert environments of Baja to give birth in winter. The whales come to Baja weighing 40 tonnes and then use about 10 tonnes of their body weight giving birth, creating milk, and using their body fat to sustain themselves— there's nothing to eat there. They lose about 10 tonnes over the course of 4 months.

While in the Baja area, they stay in the relatively sheltered, predator-free lagoons surrounded by the Baja Desert. The water is fairly warm so the youngsters require less energy to grow faster. There are three famous lagoons: Scammons Lagoon, Magdalena Bay, and San Ignacio Lagoon. We visited San

Ignacio Lagoon because of one interesting thing—whales there have become "friendly" over the past 30 years.

Years ago, researchers zipped back and forth across San Ignacio Lagoon in boats, studying and counting whales. Eventually one

BRIAN'S NOTES

Whalers would approach whales and harpoon the baby. The baby would cry for help and its mom would come in close enough for whalers to harpoon the mom. A 40-tonne angry mother is a force to be reckoned with, and many a whaler was cast into the ocean as the whales hammered their boats into splinters. That's why whalers used to call gray whales "hammerheads."

I remember photographing these blue-footed boobies when the sun illuminated them from behind. I could see bits of feathers popping off and floating in the wind like the fluff from a dandelion when you blow it.

whale came up to a boat and the researcher reached out and touched it. I guess the whale liked it, because it began meeting up with the researchers. Researchers continued these types of encounters with this whale and eventually the whale gave birth. The youngster learned the behavior as well. Other whales presumably saw these whales doing it and tried it themselves.

The news about the bizarre behavior of these unique whales spread. Some people were surprised. Gray whales had a horrible reputation because they used to smash boats and kill whalers. We don't hunt gray whales commercially anymore, so I'd like to think they've forgiven us. Now we're discovering their true nature. They are gentle giants of the ocean with brains big enough to develop a sense of curiosity. Different scientists argue about why whales come in to be touched by people, but all I can deduce is that the whales are just having fun.

Visitors are only allowed to access about 20 percent of the lagoon, and the idea is not to go looking for whales. We sat in a boat called a "panga" and waited an hour for a whale to approach. The whales have learned over the years that a boat with its engine idling is basically a signal to come and be touched. It's not like sitting around an African water hole where you have to be quiet, either. It seemed the more excited we got, the more excited the whales became. A mother came in with her calf and for a while, she kept the calf away while she enjoyed her snout massage. We also witnessed mothers

SAY THE WORD!

Annihilation: complete destruction

Ecotone: the middle ground between two environments

Keratin: the material our fingernails and hair are made from

16

coming over and holding their babies up with their snouts to allow the baby full access to the people on the boat. One baby opened its mouth and allowed Dee to stroke the baleen.

Sometimes the whales teased us. I remember reaching down and feeling like my shoulder socket was dislocating because I was straining to touch this whale that was only centimeters away from my fingers. Then the whale came up and allowed my longest finger just a quick touch before it dropped down again. That was one of

most profound experiences. It's not that I condone touching wild creatures. In fact, I'm very much hands off, but in some situations where intelligent animals seek you out to have a tactile experience, I think we can make an exception. We should also celebrate the fact that they somehow escaped total annihilation from whalers. Scientists figured gray whales would never come back because there were too few of them to survive. Fortunately, the whales proved them wrong and populations are now robust, as we saw at San Ignacio Lagoon.

The beautiful Sally Lightfoot crab lives in the intertidal zone between desert and sea in the Baja.

the first times I had ever touched a whale. Then the whale continued to pass underneath our panga for what seemed like forever, it was so long! Finally the tail fluke passed by. There were many times when I had the full flat of my hand on the whale, and its skin felt almost like vinyl. I also saw little whale lice skitter around between the barnacles on the whale's skin. Whale lice are crustaceans that hitch a ride and live on the whale. I always regretted not moving quickly enough to grab one for a closer look.

Touching wild whales was an incredible privilege and remains to this day one of my

There is an interesting cactus called creeping devil that grows horizontally like a log along the ground in the Baja Desert. It looks like a plant that has been kicked over.

LIKE TOOTHPASTE FROM THE SAND

A split second after I released the shovel-nosed lizard, it disappeared into the sand, like a fish in water. I tried to find it again, but the escape artist had vanished!

During my third trip to Africa, I visited the Namib Desert. Once again, I was the tour leader of our new "Zoofari" travel program at the Calgary Zoo. I'll never forget when we landed. We chartered an old DC3 airplane because I had a full group of 16 people with me. The size of our group allowed us to take over complete camps whenever we traveled from one place to the next, so as the trip progressed we became very close.

When we landed on the desert runway, the vehicle that came to pick us up was late. We stood under the shade of the wing, and it was blistering hot. I was scanning the horizon with my binoculars, and all I could see were heat waves shimmering in the sun. Then I saw something. The waves had fractured and magnified the image so it was almost mirage-like, but I could see a zebra shimmering in the distance.

This was a rare zebra sighting for us while we were there. More often we saw gemsbok, which are desert antelope with long straight horns. Gemsbok have an amazing ability to tolerate the heat. We sweat if our body temperature goes up because sweat evaporates and cools our body.

I've seen films showing a shovel-nosed lizard dashing across the desert sand and then picking up its legs when it stops because the sand is too hot. It looks like it's doing a strange jig. It's like the dance you would do if you stood on hot pavement in bare feet. You can almost hear the lizard saying, "Ouch, ouch" as it's picking up its feet.

18

Gemsbok are also called oryx. They can live indefinitely without water.

water currents that come up from the Antarctic and wash past the Namibian coast. The cool moist air from the ocean meets the hot air from the desert, and it condenses and creates a band of fog pretty well every morning. The sand dunes are interesting because they have specialized creatures that live on them, and some get all their moisture from this fog.

One such animal that I found fascinating was the shovel-nosed lizard. This desert lizard

Little darkling beetles hold their bums up into the desert fog, and the moisture condenses on their bodies. Then the moisture runs toward their heads and gives them a drink.

But gemsbok allow their body temperature to rise instead of sweating. If they sweat, they lose moisture, and then they'll die. Also, a gemsbok's urine is virtually nonexistent and their poop comes out as bone-dry pellets. Their nasal passages are designed so that when they exhale, any moisture that may be coming out of their lungs is reclaimed by their body. The gemsbok is a remarkable creature that is well adapted to the desert.

We went on a safari into the Namib Desert and hiked on some of the sand dunes that the desert is known for. The desert goes right to the Atlantic Ocean's edge. The Namib Desert gets some of its moisture from the cool oceanic

is adapted for escaping predation and heat by diving into the sand. Using its shovel-like nose, it burrows into the sand and disappears like a fish swimming in water. It just leaves this little squiggly trace in the sand where its tail was dragging and its toes were hitting the sand. I caught one of these lizards and had a chance to really look at it. It had fringes on its fingers and toes that allowed it to scamper across the sand with incredible efficiency.

All of the plants in the Namib Desert are sparse and tough, and have only brief opportunities to add on growth during the occasional storm. Many of them go into dormancy for years waiting for moisture, or waiting to acquire moisture from the fog. In some areas, rain hasn't fallen in hundreds of years, so it's a very dry place.

Probably one of the most remarkable plants we came across was the welwitschia plant. It looks like toothpaste squishing from the ground out of a toothpaste tube. Two leaves come out of the ground and they continue to grow and grow indefinitely. The plant becomes shredded and frayed from the whipping wind and abrasive sand. Welwitschia leaves can be meters long, but the leaves tend to curl. The ends of the leaves eventually dry out and die, but the leaves themselves continue to grow. Right where it's coming out of the ground, the green of the leaves appears

SAY THE WORD!

Abrasive: rubbing or grinding in nature

Condenses: causes a vapor to turn to liquid

Mirage: an illusion created by alternate layers of hot and cool air

translucent. It's a very pretty and very odd plant.

Every evening we set up camp in some stunning desert landscapes. Eventually, we drove into the Brandberg mountains. There we saw cave paintings left behind by some of the early San people. These 2,000-year-old paintings gave us an indication of some of the people who used

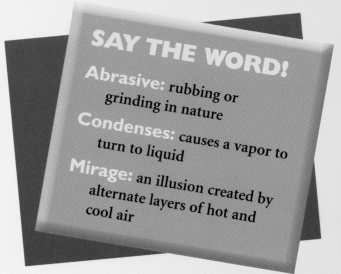

Dry river valleys like this one may not have seen flowing water for centuries. But water is often there, flowing under the sand. Desert elephants dig wells in these places, quenching their thirst and that of other animals, too.

The welwitschia plant looks a bit like a pile of trash on the desert floor. Some of these plants have lived for 1,500 years. It's like nothing I've ever seen before!

BRIAN'S NOTES

Desert elephants can survive up to 2 days without water. They go into dry river valleys and dig wells up to a couple meters deep. Water slowly percolates in, and they drink from these wells like it's liquid gold. Other creatures like baboons and antelope drink from these wells, so the elephants really are an important species. When the actions and presence of one species makes life possible for others, that species is called a keystone species. Desert elephants are a keystone species.

to live in this part of the world. We climbed some of the kopje (pronounce it like "copy") rocks in the area. These big rounded granite boulders exfoliate and break under the daytime heat and nighttime cold, so it almost looks like the gods have placed marbles on top of each other.

We saw many interesting creatures as we climbed—there were rock hyrax and plated lizards, and skinks and other creatures on these kopjes. When we reached the top, we'd watch the sun set. It was remarkable!

The Namib Desert is said to be the oldest desert on the planet. It is an amazing, ancient landscape populated by some really weird creatures and plants, all adapted to live in such a dry place.

DESERT ON ICE

A few years ago, I went to Somerset Island in the Canadian Arctic to visit my good friend Pete Jess at his ecolodge called the Arctic Watch Lodge. This was Dee's first experience in the High Arctic and I was excited to show it to her. The lodge was erected near a bay where beluga whales come every summer to perform their strange behavior of shedding their outer skin. Pete invited people to stay in comfortable tents, while being able to experience the incredible natural scene of the whales and walk the Arctic desert on Somerset.

Somerset Island provided incredible opportunities to walk! Dee and I found that the best conditions occurred between 11:00 PM and 6:00 AM We slept from 9:00 until 11:00 at night, woke up, and hiked until 4:00 or 5:00 in the morning until we were absolutely too tired to walk anymore. Then we went back to the tent and slept until 8:00 in the morning, got up for breakfast, and then hiked some more or explored the terrain with Pete in his Twin Otter aircraft.

Dee and I hiked dozens of kilometers every night. We've been hiking together a long time so we were able to cover long distances. Even though they call much of the Arctic "the Barrens," it's not barren if you look in the right places. We looked for waterfalls and ravines, and coulees and drainages to find plants and wildlife. The most interesting places involve water because in a desert environment, nothing much happens unless there's water.

One night we kept finding tufts of qiviut and piles of muskox dung on the tundra, so we knew there were muskox around. We were dead tired at 3:00 in the morning when we finally saw two little fuzzy dots on the horizon. We set up the spotting scope and, sure enough, there were muskox. We watched as 2 bull muskox showed off to each other, butting heads. It was

The tents at Arctic Watch Lodge are made of Kevlar and aluminum, which expand and contract with the temperature at exactly the same rate. They are strong tents that can withstand high winds throughout the dark, cold winter and the 24-hour-sunlight summer.

On every rock that could hold a nest, there was a Thayer's gull. This canyon we visited was a long way away from the ocean, but it gave these birds both protection from Arctic foxes, and ledges to nest on.

magnificent to see these animals strut, and then turn around and run toward each other, until their heads met with a "CRACK."

We also did some great bird-watching. There aren't that many bird species in the extreme desert of the High Arctic, but what's there is interesting. We found a ravine on a map and then we hiked toward it for what seemed like forever. On the way, we came across a red knot, which is a type of sandpiper. It feigned a broken wing, so we knew youngsters were nearby. We allowed her to lead us away from her youngsters and then we stopped and stood still like totem poles for a time. Within a few minutes, 2 chicks that looked like fuzzy golf balls with pencil legs appeared out of nowhere. They had blended perfectly into the tundra. They ran toward their mother and hid under her wings, but not before we got a look at them.

We finally made it to the ravine. The snow above the canyon was slowly melting, and this moisture was filtering through the rock walls creating an absolute oasis, Arctic-style. Everywhere there was moisture, there was thick green or red moss. It was such a contrast to the incredibly dry landscape we had hiked over to get there.

This canyon was an oasis of vegetation with lots of interesting plants and birds. Arctic plants battle dry winds, a short growing season, and permafrost. But, the permafrost is also their salvation because as the permafrost melts in the summer months, the moisture wicks up, providing needed water for the plants. To survive, these plants have to grow low to the ground. Plants often have fuzz around their stems, so they won't be desiccated by the winds that constantly pummel them.

Even though it may be just above freezing a meter above the ground, when the sun beats down, it can be much warmer right at soil level. Dee and I decided to lie on our bellies with our

During the brief Arctic summer, some melting does occur. The little rootlets of the plants that are adapted to living in cold soils pick up on that moisture. Tiny plants like this Arctic poppy have worked out how to survive in this harsh, dry, and cold environment.

Ptarmigan live on the tundra and are one of the only birds that don't migrate. They have white feathers in the winter and brown coloring in the spring and fall. They also have features on their toes that create a sort of snowshoe on their feet.

BRIAN'S NOTES

Beluga whales are the only whales to perform a catastrophic molt. About 3,000 whales come into the estuary along the northern part of Somerset Island in the High Arctic. The fresh water creates a chemical change within the skin of the whales and they exfoliate quarter-sized chunks of skin as they rub against the rocks. It's like a washing machine for whales! The skin is then consumed by the birds and ocean organisms.

Artic Watch Lodge

The main lodge at Arctic Watch Lodge is huge and comfortable with an excellent library for guests to read up on Arctic wildlife. We each had our own little tent with an oil heater, but Dee and I didn't use it. We're used to cold weather camping, and the Arctic summer temperatures dropped only to a few degrees below freezing at night. We had thick duvets and mattresses, so we felt like hibernating gophers climbing into our bed. The tents were made of white Kevlar, so it was always light inside, too. Pete Jess, the owner, had been in the Arctic for virtually all of his adult life, and had become very friendly with the local Inuit, many of whom he hired at the lodge. He's the only person who has succeeded in getting a 99-year lease on Inuit land to build the lodge. He has since sold the lodge to Arctic explorer Richard Weber.

chins on the tundra to photograph these little plants. We could actually feel the solar radiation coming off the ground. It's a whole new world down at the microlevel. There were little insects and spiders climbing around and tiny flowers taking advantage of soil-level warmth. Hummocks and little ravines create places where all-important moisture will stick around and provide a bit of nourishment for these tiny Arctic desert plants.

I find the Arctic environment thrilling because there's nobody there. In all of Nunavut, Canada, there are around 26,000 people living in just a few settlements. We flew across landscapes for hours and saw no roads or signs of human habitation.

It's just pure clean wilderness. The Canadian Arctic is a classic example of a polar desert environment, and Dee and I had a great time exploring it.

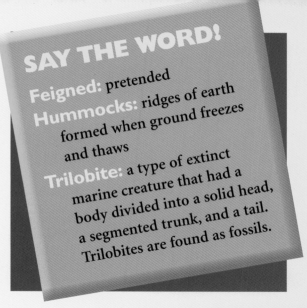

Trilobites appeared on Earth 600 million years ago. Dee and I found the best trilobite fossils we've ever seen on Somerset Island. There was once a shallow sea there—it stretched from the Gulf of Mexico all the way up to the High Arctic.

COYOTE LAUGHTER AND NEWSPAPER ROCK

When Dee and I went to Utah, we visited a series of fabulous national parks, where we did several 3- and 4-day backpacking trips. We went in the fall, which is a good time to go. In the spring and fall, temperatures are perfect for hiking, and migrating birds are moving through.

The park wardens gave us permission to camp in certain places only after they realized we weren't normal tourists. We knew how to hike in delicate landscapes without harming the environment. We hiked up a valley in a creek bed, where once a year torrential rains wash the soil away. We hiked on the slick rock, which is sandstone that is weathered over time. Dee and I walked on fairly steep slopes, yet just the traction of our sneakers or hiking boots allowed us to go almost anywhere. This way we could walk incredibly long distances without ever touching any soil.

We not only walked on the slick rock, we camped on it too. Camping on the slick rock is environmentally perfect because there are often no plants growing there to disturb. When we took our tent down, it was as if we hadn't been there: there wasn't even a footprint because there's no soil. We camped in the most amazing places—the tops of buttes, in caves with views, or on the tops of columns. And at the end of the day, Dee and I would sit and wait for the light show to begin.

I got really excited as the sun got lower on the horizon because all of a sudden this rock, which was

Rain and wind, along with the freezing and the thawing of the landscape, creates fractures and fissures that moisture can get into. Then sand storms sculpt some of the most spectacular geologic landscapes in the world.

Utah has slot
canyons. We would
have to use every
part of our bodies to crawl
and maneuver through them—
we shinnied up, climbed over,
and slithered under. We also
had to negotiate around
obstacles, and wade through
or climb around water.
It was challenging,
but exciting!

pretty during the day, would transform itself, with glowing reds, yellows, and beautiful pastels washing over amazing rock sculptures. The scene would change by the minute as the sun set. Every evening we sat with a camera handy, watching the sunset. At times, I made myself put the camera down to just drink in this incredible light show. Then it would happen again in reverse in the morning as the sun came up.

Lizards are perfectly adapted to the desert environment. With their ability to scamper across the slick rock, no insect is safe. Their mobility is the key to their survival. Even so, we did see the occasional roadrunner with a successful lizard catch.

The Utah desert was beautiful and fascinating. I remember in one park, we went into a series of canyons, some of which were very narrow. This place was like a maze. Each fissure in the ground was anywhere from 5 to 20 meters (16 to 65 ft.) deep and sometimes so narrow that Dee and I would have to turn our bodies sideways and face-forward to squeeze through. Then the slots would open up a bit and branch out in other directions. It was as if we were rats in a labyrinth following these bizarre canyons around. Anytime we felt lost or disoriented, I would shinny to the top of the canyon and look around for our tent to get my bearings. Then I'd shinny back down and we'd continue exploring. All the while, the possibility of a flash flood stayed in the back of my mind. We always had an exit strategy to get out of those slot canyons.

In the harsh deserts of Utah, it does rain after all, and we went there just after a huge rainstorm. All of the ravines and roadside ditches flowed with chocolate-colored water. Often many centimeters of rain fall in torrents in just a few hours and then nothing for months. Because of the recent rainfall, we were able to find water most everywhere we went. However, we had to assume the worst and carry water with us. We calculated how much water we'd drink, and Dee and I discovered that we each drink about 4 liters (1 gal.) a day. So for a 2-day hike, we'd carry about 9 kilograms (20 lb.) of water. Our packs were unbelievably heavy on hikes where we weren't sure we'd be able to find water.

Everywhere we went, we came across ruins of the Anasazi People who once lived in the area. We saw ancient cave paintings. This particular rock painting was called Newspaper Rock. The sites where the ruins and cave paintings were is protected, so we could look and sometimes walk into them, but we weren't allowed to touch or remove anything.

Living Soil

We met with the chief wardens in some of Utah's national parks and received special permission to hike into places they normally don't let too many people go to. Desert environments look like they should be able to withstand all kinds of abuse, and we humans have certainly abused them. It's fun to go 4x4ing or motorcycling, but the tires of these vehicles can rip up a plant that might have taken years to establish. In some parts of the Utah desert, the soil itself, called cryptobiotic soil, is also very delicate. It's actually alive, with microorganisms, algae, and fungus living within it. This cryptobiotic soil creates a net or mat on the soil, and if you step on it and break it, it can create an opening where the wind can get in, destroying what may have taken 500 years to stabilize. Cryptobiotic soils are what many park wardens and conservationists are trying to preserve in places like Utah.

Desert bats fertilize saguaro cactus flowers and many other plants as well. The bats put their tongues inside the flowers to sip nectar and accidentally collect pollen on their fuzzy faces. So, they pollinate plants as they fly from one to the next.

We hiked in these incredibly beautiful places, weighed down by heavy packs, all the while rejoicing in the life we saw around us. The plants and animals have figured out how to survive. Many plants have evolved not to have leaves, but thorns. These thorns are there to protect the fleshy interior of the plant from the ravages of creatures that want to get at the moisture. Some thorns are several centimeters long or curved like fishhooks. They can be absolutely lethal!

Other plants, like the bizarre ocotillo plant, have good survival strategies as well. The ocotillo produces fleshy leaves only when it has enough moisture to do so. When the leaves become a moisture-loss liability, the ocotillo gets rid of them and the plant goes dormant until it rains again.

We also noticed that many desert plants are silver. If you look at the leaf of a plant like the prairie silver willow under a microscope,

In Arches National Park we saw some amazing rock art carved by wind and water over millions of years.

it looks like a bunch of little umbrellas. These little silver umbrellas overlap to create a dead air space. They reflect light away from the plant and keep that subspace cooler. Humidity in this space is near 100 percent, but the hot dry wind that constantly blows can't get at this layer of moisture between the tops of the umbrellas and the leaf. This helps slow down the evapotranspiration. Also, the jade plant and other desert plants have very thick cuticle coverings almost like wax. These coverings prevent moisture from escaping from the thick and fleshy leaves. All of these strategies make for abundant plant life in this dry place.

Utah's animals are also fascinating. I'll never forget being on a high buttress in this spectacular landscape of wonderful columns, hoodoos, slick rock, and arches. We were camped under a clear starry night, and the stars looked so close, they seemed to be falling all around us. The environment was still, and the occasional call of an owl or other bird in the middle of the night echoed throughout the canyon. Then a coyote's laugh erupted from the quiet blackness. It was riveting.

> Coyotes are successful desert animals, partly because they are omnivores. They eat insects, lizards, snakes, birds, rodents, rabbits, fruit, and tortoises among other things.

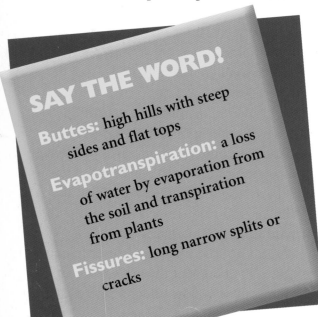

SAY THE WORD!

Buttes: high hills with steep sides and flat tops

Evapotranspiration: a loss of water by evaporation from the soil and transpiration from plants

Fissures: long narrow splits or cracks

BRIAN'S NOTES

When it rains in the desert, it usually rains hard. Then the water is gone, and the sun comes back out and dries everything out. Because of this, cacti have shallow roots to consume moisture right away. Their roots are virtually millimeters below the surface and are ready to quickly pick up the moisture. During dry times, cacti shrivel up like raisins and lose much of their rigidity. Then the rains come and, poof, they puff right back up.

During the heat of the day, it's hard to spot any wildlife. So what lives there is often nocturnal. Because of that, Dee and I did a lot of hiking at night. We wore headlamps to examine desert trees and cacti, and to look for lizards and other creatures on the ground. We became nocturnal creatures ourselves to

The ocotillo plant looks like a whole bunch of bamboo sticks growing out of the ground.

get the full meaning of what the desert is.

Night is fantastic, but dawn on the desert is beautiful, too. The temperature is cool, so it's a great time for birds to broadcast their presence. Birds perform a dawn chorus everywhere in the world, even in the desert where there aren't many bird species. Birdcalls travel the farthest at this time. The humidity at dawn, when there's no wind to blow it away and no sun to burn it away, acts as a transmitter to help the sound of the bird permeate farther across the desert environment. When the sun is coming up, I find it so exciting to lie in my tent and listen to the desert wake up. It's a polite awakening, unlike a profound tropical forest wake-up. It's clean, it's clear, it's crisp, and it's the desert at its best.

A SNAKE ESCAPE

While southern Saskatchewan and Alberta, Canada, can't be defined as classic deserts, these areas are very desert-like. They have cacti and limited rainfall. They also have the ability to evaporate more rain than ever falls and, in some areas, have classic desert animals and sand dunes. There are sand dunes in Saskatchewan that look like they're right out of the Kalahari Desert.

The first sand dunes I ever explored in Saskatchewan were the Great Sand Hills near Liebenthal, which move and shift with the wind. Because the sand allows the rain that falls, or the snow that melts, to percolate away from the evaporation zones, the water table tends to be high. This is why every sheltered area on the north side of the sand dunes hosts little groups of aspen trees, which are home to mule deer, great horned owls, and Swainson's hawks. This mixture of sand, grassland, and little pockets of trees makes for a landscape with abundant wildlife.

Canada's desert environments are fascinating. I spent a lot of time walking in Val Marie, Saskatchewan, even before it became Grasslands National Park. Dee and I would go for 3- or 4-day hikes when I was working about 90 kilometers (56 mi.) north of Swift Current, Saskatchewan, at the Prairie Wildlife Centre. We drove down on my motorcycle, set up our tent, and then hiked. We did long-distance hikes looking for cool critters. We searched for animals like horned lizards, which we never found in the

Val Marie experiences an average of 35 centimeters (14 in.) of precipitation per year, but sees less than 10 centimeters (4 in.) in times of drought. Hot days and high winds evaporate nearly twice the amount of moisture gained from precipitation.

The First Nations people had superstitions about antelope. They believed that antelope had a power to always see you before you saw them, because whenever they saw antelope, the antelope were already looking at them.

During hibernation, the body temperature of prairie dogs drops to 1 degree above the temperature of the burrow they are in.

Prairies are rolling landscapes and sometimes even rolling sand dunes, like in the Great Sand Hills in southern Saskatchewan.

wild, even though I know they live there. Once I looked back at camp with my binoculars and saw something loitering beside my motorcycle— a pronghorn antelope.

Pronghorn antelope are curious creatures, and I guess my motorcycle was nice and shiny, which intrigued it. I watched the antelope come up close and look at my motorcycle and our tent and wonder what was going on. We found a great way to attract antelope when we saw them from a distance. We'd sit down and I'd take my coat off and wave it over my head and then put it down. They'd look and look, and eventually they'd come in closer to check us out, and we'd get a good look at them.

Antelope are specialized desert animals.

They don't sweat because that would rob them of important moisture. Instead, they allow their body temperature to rise, much the same as gemsbok in Africa do. Antelope don't have to drink water either. They get their moisture from the plants they eat—some of which we consider pretty obnoxious. In winter, antelope feed almost entirely on sage, and they don't seem to mind the strong smell of the plant. The scent is so powerful because it's full of alkaloids and chemicals that slow down most

SAY THE WORD!

Alkaloids: organic, sometimes poisonous, compounds that often contain nitrogen, found mostly in plants and fungi

Hibernaculum: a shelter for a hibernating animal

33

I don't pick up rattlesnakes unless I have a good reason for doing it. I know that some of them have tricks, and even if you're holding them right, they can twist and bite you. Snakebites can be incredibly painful and potentially lethal, so I'm very careful.

animals' ability to eat it—but not antelope. The antelope will even eat cacti. They are tough animals that have evolved in a dry desert environment.

We don't have a lot of snake species in Canada, so I was excited to find rattlesnakes, racers, and bull snakes as well. I've been a snake fanatic since I was a little kid, and I find reptiles in general fascinating. In Val Marie, there were a couple amazing rattlesnake hibernaculums. I'll never forget the first time I came across one of these hibernaculums. It was in the fall when the snakes were coming back, and there were snakes everywhere. I stood in the center of the hibernaculum and counted at least 20 rattlesnakes, some of which appeared to be as thick around as my wrist. They were all

BRIAN'S NOTES

I once held a hibernating gopher. It was like a stiff fuzzy donut. When I picked it up, it started trying to wake itself up because it knew it was in danger. Gophers don't wake up often during their hibernation because waking up consumes incredible amounts of stored fat. If they wake up too often, gophers can starve to death in their sleep.

34

doing their own thing, sunning or moving around, and when I approached they would rattle their tails. It gave me a fantastic opportunity to photograph and watch them.

One year I came across a pregnant female rattlesnake. I was working with the Canadian Wildlife Service, and I captured it for study back at the Prairie Wildlife Centre. We put it on display until it gave birth. As the babies came out, they opened their mouths wide to exercise their little fangs. These pencil-thin baby snakes are fully venomous and dangerous (even at this age!). I fed them mice and then took them all to the hibernaculum in time to hibernate for the winter. I have been professionally trained to handle snakes. Even so, I do prefer to observe without disturbing them. I visited this rattlesnake hibernaculum many times just to watch and to quietly photograph. I did my best not to disturb them.

Dee and I also saw lots of blacktailed prairie dogs—after all, we camped in the middle of the only blacktailed prairie dog colony in Canada, which is in the Frenchman River Valley where Grasslands National Park is now located. Camping in a prairie dog colony was amazing because we just sat there with our binoculars and all around us were prairie dogs looking at us looking at them. After a while, they quit being freaked out by us and went about their day. They look like little butterballs because they had to put on so much fat to sustain themselves during their hibernation.

This business of hibernation is a dangerous but important tool. How else could prairie dogs

or rattlesnakes get through winters as severe as our prairie winters? I remember walking in the lower level at the Prairie Wildlife Centre, where we had floor-to-ceiling glass. I looked out into the prairies right at ground level, and I saw a weasel pulling a hibernating Richardson's Ground Squirrel, locally called a gopher, out of its burrow. The gopher was squeaking and this weasel, in a very relaxed way, slowly started to chew through the back of the gopher's neck until it stopped squeaking. This happens all winter long. Weasels and badgers make a living by finding gophers that are hibernating.

There's a whole interplay of animal life that we don't see unless we're there on a continual basis. These types of experiences just make the prairie desert come alive for Dee and me.

I have punctured so many of my mattresses on little mammalaria cacti because they are so well camouflaged in the grass. Now, before I put my mat down, I pat all over with my hands to make sure none are there.

UPSIDE-DOWN GALAHS DOWN UNDER

Dee and I spent about 2 months in Australia. We were told how vast the desert is, and I was expecting to see miles of nothing. When we got there, there were miles of everything. On bus trips, every time we stopped for gas, Dee and I would hop out and run around bird-watching like crazy. Then we would sit with our bird books and try to identify what we had seen. There's an amazing amount of life if you know how and where to look.

At night, I would sit with the driver and watch what the headlights picked up. We saw kangaroos, snakes, and other interesting creatures on the side of the road. I was just dying to have the bus driver slam on the brakes so I could go out and photograph the critters that were scampering off the road.

We finally got off the bus in Alice Springs. I remember waking up in our campground and walking downtown to rent a car. We encountered a group of probably 50 galahs, which are pink parrots, on a telephone line. Dee and I stood there in amazement as we watched these birds. They'd look at the bird to the left and the bird to the right, and then fall straight ahead holding on to the wire with their feet and hang upside down. They'd let their wings droop above their heads, and they would cackle with laughter. Parrots have a sense of humor and they were having fun. There's no other way to explain what they were doing—they were just goofing off. We stood there laughing out loud at these silly birds.

We finally left the galahs and rented a car to drive out into the Simpson Desert to Ellery Gorge. We decided to camp on the other side of this gorge so we had to carry our gear above

During the heat of the day we would often find shade and watch birds like Port Lincoln parrots come down and drink at the water. We'd also watch zebra finches and red-tailed cockatoos fly in. The bird life is amazing in the Australian Outback, especially around a place like Ellery Gorge, where they all come to drink.

This was a sad moment for me, as I found this galah on the ground with a broken wing. We were in such a remote area that we could not help this poor bird. Nature can be cruel, but it's all a part of the bigger picture. I'm sure a dingo or a hawk eventually found the parrot.

We were always dealing with the flies. They loved the moisture and salt on our skin from sweating. The outback handshake is a wave in front of the face to shoo away flies. As soon as the sun went down the flies would disappear. It was such a relief!

our heads across the water. This was tricky because it's very tough swimming across a deep cold gorge with one hand over your head. We made several trips, but it was worth it. We loved the isolation of being on the other side with the big red cliffs towering above us on each side.

We swam in the gorge day and night. I remember looking up from the still water at night, the black silhouettes of the cliffs outlined above by the most incredible chandelier of stars. Australia is in the southern hemisphere, so we enjoyed a sense of discovery as we tried to get to know a completely different set of constellations, including the famous Southern Cross.

Each day we arose at the crack of dawn and hiked until about 10:00 in the morning until the heat was too intense. It was like hiking in a pizza oven! We had to walk very slowly and carefully because the spinifex grass has long, very tough leaves—it's just like grass filled with spikes, and it would easily pierce your skin right through your socks and running shoes. We climbed to the top of one of the ridges in the Simpson Desert and saw

SAY THE WORD!

Canid: members of the canine family, including wolves, foxes, jackals, and coyotes

Ecologists: biologists who study the relationship between organisms and their environment

Gorge: a cleft in a valley, or a place where the earth has parted and created a deep water hole

Marginal environment: a part of the world that receives only 31–41 centimeters (12–16 in.) of rain per year

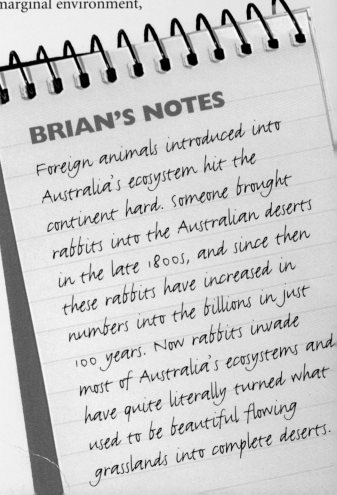

Dee and I came across wild camels brought to the Simpson Desert from Arabia. Camels have all kinds of adaptations that allow them to survive in deserts—their noses close down, they recycle water and can go for long periods of time without water, and they store water in the fat of their humps.

Wildlife in Australia is exciting. Australia has been separated from other continents for so long that it has a variety of animal forms that are very different from those found any other place on earth. Where else can you see huge mouse-shaped animals called kangaroos hopping around with pouches on their bellies? What a bizarre animal! A kangaroo gives birth to an immature little peanut of a baby called a joey. A joey is about the size of a cashew nut when it's born. After it's born, it squiggles up like a pink worm to the mother's pouch and climbs in. It finds the nipple, which begins to swell into the shape of a light bulb inside the little baby's mouth so it can't pull off.

Once it attaches itself to the nipple, the joey begins to eat and grow. Because they live in a marginal environment,

beautiful rolling hills stretching all the way to the horizon and the soft pastel colors of the exposed bedrock of the desert.

It was a feast for the ears, as we were greeted by the sounds of birds, like zebra finches, calling. We saw and heard many interesting birds that are only found in these desert environments.

One time, when we were working our way down a cliff after bird-watching and hiking, we came across a whole herd of wild horses called brumbies. To a horse lover, this is exciting, but as ecologists we know they don't belong there. Brumbies were domestic horses at one time, but now they run wild in the outback of Australia.

BRIAN'S NOTES

Foreign animals introduced into Australia's ecosystem hit the continent hard. Someone brought rabbits into the Australian deserts in the late 1800s, and since then these rabbits have increased in numbers into the billions in just 100 years. Now rabbits invade most of Australia's ecosystems and have quite literally turned what used to be beautiful flowing grasslands into complete deserts.

I was able to photograph this tiny baby kangaroo in its mother's pouch because one of the zookeepers at the Calgary Zoo has a very special relationship with the kangaroos in his care. He was able to carefully open the pouch for me to take a photograph. Wallabies, such as the mother and joey in the picture to the right, also carry their babies in pouches.

kangaroos only invest about 30 days' worth of energy into producing a baby. If the baby is born in drought conditions, all the mother kangaroo has to do is reach into her pouch, pull the baby off the nipple, and throw it away to stop it from sapping all of her energy. Then she survives and has an opportunity to produce another baby when conditions improve. When conditions are good, she can have a baby developing in the womb, a baby in the pouch growing into a beautiful little joey, and another joey that has been kicked out of the pouch but still sticks its head in every so often for a drink. Kangaroos can be baby factories.

Seeing the kangaroos, galahs, brumbies, camels, and other amazing creatures in the beautiful Simpson Desert was incredible. Our trip to Australia was the first of many really spectacular desert experiences.

Some deserts are extremely harsh with rolling sand dunes, but they are fairly rare. Most deserts have a lot of highly developed, highly specialized vegetation that is able to survive in the mostly dry conditions, and the Simpson Desert is one of those places.

RETURNING NATURE'S CATTLE

Outside of the established national parks, southern Zimbabwe was once populated by natural wildlife that had existed there for millennia. There were more than a dozen species of antelope, and there were elephants, giraffes, buffalo, and baboons. With some animals grazing coarse grass, some eating new shoots, some eating leaves, and others eating stems or stripping bark, all of the animals could coexist. There was no competition for food. In addition, keystone species like elephants would keep the trees under control by pushing them down, creating a mix of forest and grassland. And predators, like lions, would help to keep animal populations in balance.

However, in the mid-1960s, the Zimbabwean government decided to open southern Zimbabwe up to ranching. The first ranchers returned to the government and said, "This is great, but we cannot build a ranch in a zoo." The government responded by sending out national parks staff to shoot the wild animals, including all the elephants that were interfering with the new ranches. The ranch fences went up and huge numbers of cattle were brought in. Soon, very little of the original wildlife existed in the area at all.

Because southern Zimbabwe is a marginal landscape—a part of the world that receives only 31–41 cm (12–16 in.) of rain per year—the ranchers

Today, many of Africa's big animals live together at the Savé Valley Conservancy in southern Zimbabwe. Elephants, hippos, and of course, the lanky giraffe all share this space a man named Clive Stockil reclaimed for them.

couldn't support that many cattle. She slammed the door in 1992 with one of the worst droughts southern Zimbabwe had seen in 500 years.

Winds came in and swept away the topsoil, trees fell over because roots were exposed, and water holes and springs that were normally moist all year dried up completely. The landscape changed drastically. All the cows died and the ranches completely collapsed. About 20 ranchers who owned over a million hectares of cattle country went broke. The land seemed to be completely destroyed, and many people in Zimbabwe thought it would take at least 100 years to recover.

Zebras will eat both tall and short grasses, even bark and roots in times of drought. Their dependence on water, though, means they do not wander farther than 10-12 km (6-7 mi.) from water.

I was in Zimbabwe in 1992 during the drought and I remember seeing domestic goats up in the trees, eating the buds! I later visited a park called Gonarezhou, where many of the elephants and hippos perished during the drought. It was here that I first met Clive Stockil, who told me that he used a bulldozer to dig into the river bed, trying to keep some water available for the elephants and hippos. He said that as he sat and worked on his bulldozer, a lineup of elephants would form behind him, waiting for him to finish so they could drink.

Clive Stockil was one of the ranchers who lost all his cattle in the drought. Today, he's the main reason that this part of southern Zimbabwe isn't a wasteland still. He was born and raised in southern Zimbabwe and remembered what it was like when he was a kid with all the wild animals around. Because of this childhood memory, he had a vision, and he acted on it.

Baobab trees like this one can grow up to 25 meters (82 ft.) tall and live for several thousand years. The largest baobab tree in southern Africa is 46.8 meters (152 ft.) around!

BRIAN'S NOTES

In some parts of Africa, elephants repopulate forests by eating seeds and depositing them elsewhere in their dung. In areas where elephants have been eliminated, species of trees have disappeared. It can seem that elephants are destroying the forest, but they're not. They're changing, maintaining, and replanting the forest, ensuring that a diversity of plants and animals can live there. Of course, an area that is overpopulated by elephants can become a big problem.

remembered what it was like when he was a kid with all the wild animals around. Because of this childhood memory, he had a vision, and he acted on it. He proposed getting rid of all the fences, and building just one perimeter fence and restocking the area with the animals that the government had wiped out years earlier.

This vision became the Savé Valley Conservancy. He got the ranchers to cooperate because they had nothing to lose. All they had left was a dried out chunk of range land. He also got the people living in the villages in the area on board by asking them to think about wildlife in a different way.

Clive met with village elders and leaders in the surrounding districts and asked for their cooperation. He told them that he wanted to bring back the

Part of what spurred Clive Stockil on to create the conservancy was the threat against the black rhinoceros. It was being poached into extinction! Now the Savé Valley Conservancy is working to protect these massive creatures.

Clive Stockil supports the Lowveldt Wild Dog Project, which studies the behavior and ecology of a population of African Wild Dogs. In this picture, Dee looks on as Clive uses radio telemetry to track the wild dogs in the conservancy.

antelope, the giraffes, the hippos and elephants, and that he needed their help. Clive knew that they valued their cattle as we would value a rich bank account—so he asked them to think about the wildlife as "Nature's Cattle." Some of them might have stripes, funny horns, spots, or long noses, but they were as important to Nature as the villagers' cattle were to them.

If Clive was going to start bringing in "Nature's Cattle", the local people had to accept the creatures, with their stripes and spots and spiral horns. Clive suggested that if they didn't go in and poach these animals, he could eventually build up a healthy population. He convinced them that "Nature's Cattle" could be their cattle, too. Healthy populations meant people could go in each year and harvest a percentage of the animals for meat. A few hunters could come in from elsewhere in the world and pay large sums of money to trophy hunt, too. This money would

Moving a Herd of Elephants

All the old baobab trees in the Savé Valley Conservancy show that there were always elephants in the area. You see, a baobab keeps track of history by what happens to its bark, and the baobabs in the conservancy are covered in scars from where elephants have tusked apart the trees. Clive Stockil knew he had to bring in about 1,000 elephants to maintain the delicate balance of life in the park. Moving this many elephants had never been done before. This is how he did it.

After negotiating with national parks in the area, Clive would get together about 100 people to move a herd of female elephants. They would find a group of about 15 to 25. A helicopter would then go in, and an expert would tranquilize the matriarch, or lead female, and wait for her to fall. The elephants in the herd would gather around her and not move; they would wait with their leader. The people in the helicopter would then let the truck team know that they could go in. The trucks were special ones, known as "bundu bashers." Equipped with big steel bumpers that allowed them to crash through trees as thick around as your leg, the trucks would move in, with many of the trees bouncing back up behind them.

After all of the elephants (except for the babies) were tranquilized, people would move quickly to roll the elephants onto rubber mats attached to the big trucks. Then the mats would be rolled in, like big rubber tongues, until the elephants were inside the open-to-the-air truck containers. Quickly, making sure that the elephants weren't tranquilized for too long in the heat of the sun, a veterinarian would go around and wake up each elephant with an antidote shot in the biggest vein of each elephant's ear. Slowly, the elephants would awake. They would be relaxed but curious, and their trunks would slowly snake out of the holes in the containers, where they would find buckets of water to refresh them.

Then, the "bundu bashers" would be off again, returning to the conservancy. Once back, they would release the elephants into

a big stockade called a boma. Here the elephants would rest until midnight that night. At midnight, the door to the boma would be opened, and they would be free to wander out into the night of their new home. By morning, the herd would be gone from the boma.

A New York writer once wanted to know what happened to the elephants after midnight. With Clive, she sat on a platform above the gate to the boma. They waited, with nothing happening except for some rumblings in the night, until about 2:00 AM. Then, a big bull elephant came into the boma from outside, found the matriarch, wrapped his trunk around hers, and led her (with the rest of the elephants following) out into the conservancy. I'd like to think that he had heard the elephants rumbling and came in to reassure them, to let them know that he was okay and that they would be okay, too.

When we went to the grinding mill, we saw people walking in with big buckets of raw grain. They walked out a few minutes later with pure white corn flour.

be used to build things like flour mills so the women wouldn't have to spend a full day every week grinding corn with a mortar and pestle. The money could also be used to set up clinics so diseases like malaria could be treated appropriately and doctors and nurses could be brought in. Some of that money would also be used to keep the wildlife in the conservancy healthy.

Clive negotiated with national parks that had large populations of animals, and brought in hundreds of elephants and thousands of antelope, buffalo, and giraffes. The first animals Clive brought to the conservancy were black rhinoceroses, which were being poached in the Zambezi Valley. Clive went on to prove that you could take an area overpopulated with elephants and transport an entire herd by truck. The Savé Valley Conservancy became home to many grazing animals as well as the rare African Wild Dog. Essentially, Clive put back what Nature originally had in place!

A year after Clive started to bring back the landscape, Nature smiled on him and gave him abundant rains. Lakes that had virtually dried up filled again. Clive's dream came true. I had dinner with Clive Stockil in 2004, and he told me that the Savé Valley Conservancy was going strong.

The desertification of more and more land in the world is a force to be reckoned with, and steps must be taken to prevent it. Just look at the Sahel—the harsh landscape is already pushing people out. I find it amazing that people survive there, anyway. But if we're ingenious enough to survive in these harsh environments, certainly we must be able to begin preventing desertification, just as Clive Stockil did in southern Zimbabwe.

CONSERVATION—IT'S UP TO YOU!

If you'd like to learn more about or become involved in wildlife conservation, contact any or all of the following organizations.

African Conservation Foundation
African office: PO Box 11577
Meru, Arusha, Tanzania
255-744-65-3881

UK Office: PO Box 36
Bingley, W. Yorkshire
BD16 1LQ   UK
44-0-1535-274-160
www.africanconservation.org

Calgary Zoo
1300 Zoo Road, SE
Calgary, AB T2E 7V6
1-403-232-9333
www.calgaryzoo.ab.ca

Canadian Parks and Wilderness Society
National Office
880 Wellington Street, Suite 506
Ottawa, Ontario K1R 6K7
info@cpaws.org 1-800-333-WILD
www.cpaws.org

Canadian Nature Federation
1 Nicholas Street, Suite 606
Ottawa, Ontario K1N 7B7
cnf@cnf.ca 1-613-562-3447
www.cnf.ca

Canadian Wildlife Federation
350 Michael Cowpland Drive
Kanata, Ontario K2M 2W1
info@cwf-fcf.org 1-800-563-WILD
www.cwf-fcf.org

Chihuahuan Desert Research Institute
Box 905
Fort Davis, Texas 79734
(432) 364-2499
manager@cdri.org   www.cdri.org

David Suzuki Foundation
2211 West 4th Avenue, Suite 219
Vancouver, BC V6K 4S2
solutions@davidsuzuki.org
1-800-453-1533
www.davidsuzuki.org

Desert Foothills Land Trust
PO Box 4861
Cave Creek, Arizona 85327
info@dflt.org
www.dflt.org/index.htm

Ducks Unlimited (Wetland Conservation)
Box 1160
Oak Hammock Marsh, Manitoba R0C 2Z0
1-800-665-3835 www.ducks.ca

The Jane Goodall Institute (Canada)
Mr. Nicolas Billon, Executive Assistant
P. O. Box 477, Victoria Station
Westmount, Quebec H3Z 2Y6
nicolas@janegoodall.ca 1- 514-369-3384 (fax)
www.janegoodall.ca

Marmot Recovery Foundation
Marmot
Box 2332, Station A
Nanaimo, BC V9R 6X9
1-877-4MARMOT www.marmots.org

Savé Valley Conservancy
Private Bag 7032
Chiredzi
Zimbabwe
info@savevalleyconservancy.com
+263 1 141 2271
www.savevalley.net

Cool Sites on the Web:
Species At Risk: www.speciesatrisk.ca
Space for Species: www.spaceforspecies.ca
Arizona–Sonora Desert Museum:
www.desertmuseum.org

A free Teacher's Guide
is available for this book
at: http://www.fitzhenry.
ca/guides.htm
or call 1-800-387-9776.

46

Africa: Angola, 11; Botswana, 10–13; Johannesburg, 11; Namibia, 18–21; Sahel, 45; Zimbabwe, 40–45

Anasazi People, 28

antelope: gemsbok/oryx, 18–19; pronghorn, 33

Arabia, 38

Artic fox, 23

Arctic poppy, 24

Artic Watch Lodge, 22, 25

Arizona, 6–9 (and Tucson, 6)

Arizona Desert Museum, 6

Australia, 36–39 (and Alice Springs, 36; Ellery Gorge, 36–37; Simpson Desert, 36–39)

baboon, 21, 40

baleen, 14, 15

barnacle, 17

beetles: darkling, 19

birds: acorn woodpecker, 6; booby, 14, 16; elf owl, 9; frigate, 14; galah, 36, 37, 39; great horned owl, 32; hornbill, 12; Port Lincoln parrot, 36; ptarmigan, 24; red knot, 23; roadrunner, 6–7, 27; Swainson's hawk, 32; Thayer's gull, 23; zebra finch, 36, 38

black rhinoceros, 43, 45

boma, 45

Botswana, 10–13 (and Chobe National Park, 12; Kalahari Desert, 10–13; Maun, 11; Moremi, 12; Okavango Delta, 10–13; Okavango River, 10–13; Savuti, 12)

brumby, 38

buffalo, 40, 45

Calgary Zoo, 5, 6, 18, 39 (and ZooFari, 18)

camel, 38

Canada: Alberta, 4, 32; Beaufort Sea, 15; Mackenzie Delta, 10; Saskatchewan, 4–5, 32–35; Somerset Island, Nunavut, 22–25

cheetah, 13

coyote, 30, 37

crocodile, 10

cryptobiotic soil, 29

drought, 32, 39, 41

elephant, 11, 12, 13, 20, 21, 40–45

gecko, 7

giraffe, 11, 12, 13, 40, 43, 45

hippo, 10, 13, 40, 41, 43

Jess, Pete, 22, 25

kangaroo, 36, 38–39

lion, 12, 40, 41

lizards: plated, 21; shovel-nosed, 18, 19–20; zebra-tailed, 7

malaria, 45

Mexico, 14–17 (and Baja Desert, 14–17; Magdalena Bay, 15; San Ignacio Lagoon, 15–17; Scammons Lagoon, 15)

millipede, 7

mule deer, 32

Namibia, 18–21 (and Brandberg Mountains, 20–21; Namib Desert, 18–21)

plants: barrel cactus, 8; corn, 45; creeping devil, 17; mammalaria cacti, 35; ocotillo, 29, 31; papyrus, 13; sage, 33–34; saguaro cactus, 8, 29; spinifex, 37; welwitschia, 20, 21

qiviut, 22, 23

rabbit, 30, 38

rattlesnake, 34–35

rock hyrax, 21

rodents: badger, 35; black-tailed prairie dog, 35; gopher, 25, 34, 35; prairie dog, 33, 35; Richardson's Ground Squirrel, 35; weasel, 35

Sally Lightfoot crab, 17

Saskatchewan, 4–5, 32–35 (and Frenchman River Valley, 35; Grasslands National Park, 32, 35; Great Sand Hills, 32; Liebenthal, 32; Prairie Wildlife Centre, 4–5, 32, 35; Swift Current, 4–5, 32; Val Marie, 32, 34)

scorpion, 7

sea lion, 14

skink, 21

sow bug, 7

Stockil, Clive, 40, 41, 43, 44, 45

trees: aspen, 32; baobab, 42, 44; sausage, 13

United States: Arizona, 6–9; Mississippi Delta, 10; San Diego, 14; Utah, 26–31

Weber, Richard, 25

whale lice, 17

whales: beluga, 22, 24; gray, 14–17

whaling, 15, 16, 17

zebra, 18, 40–41

Zimbabwe, 40–45 (and Gonarezhou, 41; Savé Valley Conservancy, 40–45)

I saw this painted reed frog in Zimbabwe when Dee and I were exploring the rivers and springs there. Join me in my next book, *Amazing Animal Adventures in Rivers*, and I'll introduce you to the world of rivers and the animals that live near them and in them!

Cover and interior design by John Luckhurst
Cover and interior photographs by Brian and Dee Keating
Edited by Rennay Craats
Copyedited by Kirsten Craven
Scans by ABL Imaging

The publisher gratefully acknowledges the support of the Canada Council for the Arts and the Department of Canadian Heritage.

THE CANADA COUNCIL | LE CONSEIL DES ARTS
FOR THE ARTS | DU CANADA
SINCE 1957 | DEPUIS 1957

We acknowledge the financial support of the Government of Canada through the Book Publishing Industry Development Program (BIPDP) for our publishing activities.

Printed in China

05 06 07 08 09 / 5 4 3 2 1

First published in the United States in 2006 by Fitzhenry & Whiteside
121 Harvard Avenue, Suite 2
Allston, MA 02134

Library and Archives Canada Cataloguing in Publication

Keating, Brian, 1955-
Amazing animal adventures in the desert / with Brian Keating

(Going wild)
Includes index.
ISBN 1-894856-71-6 (bound).—ISBN 1-894856-724 (pbk.)

1. Desert animals—Juvenile literature. I. Title.
II. Series: Keating, Brian, 1955- . Going wild.

QL116.K42 2005   j591.754
C2005-902380-5

FIFTH HOUSE LTD.
A Fitzhenry & Whiteside Company
1511, 1800-4 St. SW
Calgary, Alberta T2S 2S5

1-800-387-9776
www.fitzhenry.ca

ACKNOWLEDGEMENTS

There are many people who have inspired me in my work as a naturalist. I would like to thank: Allan Morgan of Tucson, who was the first professional naturalist to take me into the magical world of the desert, giving me some new understandings of what "dry" means; the McLean and Richard families of Australia, who took us in and treated us like family on some amazing outback desert explorations; my good friends Eric Kuhn and Sue Webb, who inspired our travels into the deserts of Utah and Arizona; Bob Peart and Alex Zellermeyer, who believed enough in my abilities as a naturalist to hire me as one of the team at the Prairie Wildlife Centre so many years ago; Pete Jess, who treated me to an exquisite Arctic desert experience at Arctic Watch on Somerset Island; and Colin Bell and his professionals, who run Wilderness Safaris in Southern Africa. A special thanks to Clive Stockil in Zimbabwe, one of the most visionary and courageous conservationists I have ever met. All of you have given me such inspiration and insight into what life is all about in the driest parts of the world. Thank you, too, to the Calgary Zoo, for enabling my childhood dreams of exploring the world's wild areas (including deserts) to come true. And thanks to the people who have come on "ZooFari" trips with me: you have been wonderful traveling companions.

Most important, I would like to thank my wife Dee, who shares my love for these desert regions and who is my dedicated travel partner.

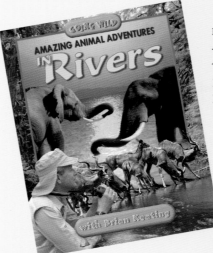